#2

HITTY'S TRAVELS

Gold Rush Days

ELLEN WEISS

ILLUSTRATED BY BETINA OGDEN

ALADDIN PAPERBACKS

New York   London   Toronto   Sydney   Singapore

This book is a work of fiction. Any references to historical events, real people, or real locales are used fictitiously. Other names, characters, places, and incidents are the product of the author's imagination and any resemblance to actual events or locales or persons, living or dead, is entirely coincidental.

First Aladdin Paperbacks edition November 2001

Text copyright © 2001 by Simon & Schuster
Illustrations copyright © 2001 by Betina Ogden

Aladdin Paperbacks
An imprint of Simon & Schuster
Children's Publishing Division
1230 Avenue of the Americas
New York, NY 10020

Designed by Debra Sfetsios
The text of this book was set in Celestia Antiqua

Printed and bound in the United States of America

2 4 6 8 10 9 7 5 3 1
Library of Congress Control Number: 2001046168
ISBN 0-689-84677-0

CHAPTER ONE

My Adventure Begins

"Papa, she's so pretty! May I have her? Really?"

It was not the first time I had heard words like these. It was not to be the last, either. But the words were very welcome on this snowy fourth day of February 1849. I did not know then that I was about to begin a great adventure.

Perhaps I had better introduce myself to you, dear reader. My name is Hitty, short for Mehitabel. I was carved by an old peddler in the state of Maine. He made me for a girl named Phoebe. Phoebe had loved me very much. With red thread, she had embroidered my name—

HITTY—onto my slip. And there it still was, though Phoebe had long since grown up. Anyone who looked at me closely could learn my name.

I had been sitting on the shelf of Mr. Harper's Curiosity Shop for several months. My blue satin dress was matted, my hair was full of dust, and I was not in good company. I was propped in between a pair of nasty china pug dogs.

The little girl who stood before me looked to be about ten. She had wildly curly brown hair, barely kept in check by a white ribbon. Her eyes were as dark as shoe buttons, and her cheeks were pink. She was not the kind of girl who could hold still for long.

"Can we afford her, Papa?" she asked.

"Well," he said, "I said you could have a new doll for our journey, and a new doll you'll have."

Annie threw her arms around her father's

neck and hugged him. "She will be such good company on the way to California!" she said.

"I only wish your mother could be with us," he said sadly.

"She will be with us," said Annie. "She'll be looking down from heaven."

Her father patted her on the head. "Right you are," he said. "Right you are."

And that was how I came to belong to Miss Annie Brown of New York City. The Browns lived in a comfortable home on West Tenth Street. Mr. Simon Brown taught English at Miss Harper's School for Young Ladies. This meant that Annie's education there was free. Someday, he hoped to open his own school.

But that life was about to change. Annie and her father were going to join the great Gold Rush. It had all begun the year before. In 1848, a gold nugget the size of a dime had been found in

California. But that tiny rock was enough to start an avalanche of events. A few men from nearby San Francisco went to investigate. They returned with their pockets full of gold. Now everyone was crazy for gold. "GOLD!" screamed the headlines in the *New York Herald*. "HO! FOR CALIFORNIA!"

Wild stories raced around. There were tales of golden boulders, too big to carry. The streams held so many nuggets, you just had to bend down to fill your pockets. Even the streets, it was said, were lined with gold. All kinds of people rushed to California. They were farmers and bankers. They were waiters, slaves and freed slaves, and ministers. They came from as far away as China and France. They were already being called forty-niners: the miners of 1849.

Annie's mother had died the year before. She had gotten influenza, and the doctors could not save her. Mr. Brown was trying to stay cheerful for Annie, but it was hard. I could see it in his dark eyes from the moment I met him. It seemed to me that he wanted to leave New York because he wanted to start fresh. His house was filled with his wife's pretty touches. He wanted to be in a place that had no memories for him.

Annie was a girl with a happy nature. Even though she was grieving for her mother, she tried to cheer her father up.

"Papa," she would say, "play the piano for me. I'll sing a song." He would smile and sit down on the shiny black bench. Annie would sit me on top of the piano while she sang. The piano vibrated my whole body.

Annie had the most beautiful voice I had ever heard. She sounded like a little angel. Sometimes she would sing old songs, like "Yankee Doodle" and "Home, Sweet Home." I had heard both songs before, but "Home, Sweet Home" touched my heart in a new way. I saw

her father's eyes fill up when Annie sang this verse:

"I gaze on the moon as I tread the drear wild,
And feel that my mother now thinks of her child . . .
Be it ever so humble, there's no place like home."

And then, to cheer him up a bit, Annie talked him into singing the popular songs of the day. So many were being written about the Gold Rush! There was one I liked especially. It went at a very good speed, and it had a catchy tune. The first verse went this way:

"Come all ye poor men of the north
who are working for your lives,
For to support your families, your children
and your wives.
There is easier ways of gaining wealth
than toiling night and day;

Go and dig the gold that lies in Californ-i-ay!"

I must admit, I was very excited to be going to California. It was going to be the greatest adventure a doll ever had. And perhaps we would find gold right away!

CHAPTER TWO

Ready, Set . . .

Mr. Brown wanted to leave as soon as possible. But there was a lot to do. The first thing was to decide how we would get there. There were three ways to do it. None of them were easy. Every night, Annie and her father studied newspapers, magazines, and advertisements.

One way was to travel west over land. The jumping-off point was Missouri. Thousands of families gathered on the banks of the Missouri River, waiting for spring. While they waited, they outfitted themselves for the long, hard trip. They bought covered wagons and teams of oxen

or mules to pull them. Then they needed food, pots and pans, medicines, seeds, guns, bedding, and more. All this was very, very expensive.

The trip was terribly hard: two thousand miles with no roads. There were rivers to cross, with no bridges over them. There were mountains to climb, and a sweltering desert to cross. There were Indians who did not like their homelands being invaded. Out on the prairie, the wind howled all night, and so did the wolves. If people were lucky, the trip took about eight months. If they were unlucky, they did not get to California alive at all.

Another way to travel was by boat. There were two main routes. You could book passage on a ship that was sailing all the way around Cape Horn. It cost about two hundred dollars. Cape Horn was the southern tip of South America, almost the bottom of the world. The trip could take a year. A year on a cramped boat, tossed by waves and storms.

The third way was to shorten the boat trip by cutting across Panama. The country of Panama was a skinny little strip of land between North America and South America.

"Look here, Annie," said her father. He pointed to an advertisement in the newspaper. "THE EASY WAY TO CALIFORNIA!" it said. "A PLEASANT TRIP! ONLY FIVE WEEKS FROM NEW YORK TO SAN FRANCISCO!" It had a picture of a splendid steamship in the center.

"That does sound a lot better than a year on a boat, Papa," said Annie. "But, how does the ship get across Panama?"

"It explains it here," he replied. He pointed to the bottom of the advertisement.

"A quick voyage to northern Panama," he read. "Then, a scenic journey of five days across the land, to Panama City. Modern ships will be waiting there to carry passengers north to San Francisco."

"It sounds so much better than the other ways!" said Annie.

"I think so, too," her father said.

"How much does it cost?" Annie bent over the ad again, and her face fell. "It's three hundred and fifty dollars each."

Mr. Brown put his hand on her curly head. "Don't you worry about that," he said. "We'll find the money. I'll sell most of what we have. We can't take it with us, anyway. Besides," he added, "I went to hear a gentleman named Mr. Atherton speak last week. He's just returned from California. Miners are making a thousand dollars a day there, he said."

"Oh, my goodness!" said Annie.

"So," he went on, "when we come back, we can buy all new things. Even if Atherton is wrong by half, we will still make more money every day than I make in months here."

"Then it's Ho for California!" she said.

CHAPTER THREE

. . . Go!

The next few weeks were a whirl of activity. Mr. Brown sold almost everything they owned. The house was filled with people, looking around as if they were in a furniture shop. At these times, Annie stayed in her room with me. "I hope we're doing the right thing," she said to me. "It will be fun to go on an adventure, but . . ." She looked around. "I'll miss this room," she said. "I'll miss my bed. I'll miss my writing-desk. It's a good thing I can take you." She kissed me on the cheek.

There was one thing that Annie was planning

on taking along, though. It was a pretty red silk bag that came all the way from China. It had belonged to her mother. "After all," she told her father, "I must have something to put my gold in."

Mr. Brown laughed. "Perhaps you will make us rich, Annie," he said.

One evening, a tall man was talking to Mr. Brown in the parlor when Annie and I went downstairs. "How much for the piano?" the man was saying.

The piano, I knew, was the finest thing the Browns owned. I hoped that Mr. Brown would get a good price for it.

"Five hundred dollars," said Mr. Brown.

"Five hundred dollars!" the man repeated. "Why, that's outrageous! I'll give you two hundred."

"It is a very good piano," said Mr. Brown firmly. "If you can find one as good for less, I urge you to buy it."

Everyone stood very still. Annie hardly breathed.

"All right," said the man at last. "Five hundred. But it's robbery."

Mr. Brown just smiled politely as the man wrote out the check. When the man was gone, he shut the door carefully. He waited a moment. Then he let out a great whoop of joy.

"Five hundred dollars!" he cried. "I never in my wildest dreams thought I could get that much for it!"

Annie ran to him and hugged him. "That's almost our passage on the ship right there!" she said. "You were such a good salesman!"

"I was shaking in my boots," he confessed.

At last, it was all done. The house was empty, and the keys had been given back to the landlady. A horse-drawn cab was waiting to take them to the dock.

Annie stood by the door, taking a last look around. Around her wrist was the red silk bag. "Good-bye, house," she whispered. "Good-bye, New York."

Then they closed the door and walked out to the cab.

The docks were a madhouse. Beside every pier, there was a ship waiting to take on passengers. Excited people rushed in all directions. There was a huge *tooot* from their ship's smokestack.

We made our way up the gangplank. Annie held on to me very tightly and tried not to look down at the water. At the top, a man waited to take our tickets.

"You're in luck," he said to Mr. Brown. "Only four people in your room."

Mr. Brown's face fell. "Four people!" he cried. "I paid for a room for two of us!"

The man gave a short laugh. "Boat's too crowded for that sort of thing," he said. "Do you want to go to California or not?"

"It will be all right, Papa," said Annie. "Maybe the boat from Panama to California will be better."

Her father sighed. "I suppose we have no choice," he said. "Annie, you're a plucky girl."

"*All aboard!*" shouted a sailor above us.

The trip to Panama was one of the least pleasant journeys I have ever had. We hit some bad weather off the Carolinas, and the boat pitched and heaved for days. Annie could not eat a thing. She looked green.

Our roommates were two young men, off to make their fortunes. Their names were James and Arthur. They were as polite as could be. When it was time for Annie to get dressed, they were happy to leave the cabin.

We were soon to learn how few women and children were traveling to California. Annie and two little boys were the only children on the boat. Sad to say, the boys were not good company at all. They ran wild from one end of the boat to the other, yelling and banging things. Annie and I avoided them at all costs.

The only woman on the whole boat was the boys' mother. She looked cross all the time. Annie called her "the sour apple." Of course, if I had had to be the mother of those boys, I would have been a sour apple, too.

After two weeks, we steamed into the port of Colón. It was a small town, and surely a quiet one before the Gold Rush. The people here spoke Spanish. *Colón,* I learned, meant "Columbus."

As soon as the gangplanks were down, everyone rushed off our boat. Annie jumped up and down ten times, she was so happy to be on solid ground. I was just as happy as she was.

As the luggage was unloaded, some passengers began ordering around the town's inhabitants. "You, there!" one of them shouted. "Carry these bags to the hotel." Some of the townspeople simply stared. Others were happy to make some extra money. But I was embarrassed at how the American men treated the foreigners.

Meanwhile, Mr. Brown was speaking quietly with a man nearby. "To go to Panama City," the man said in a heavy accent, "you have to take a boat. It's called a bungo. I can carry eight people. At the end of the river, you walk."

"How much will it cost?"

"Forty dollars for you. Twenty for the little girl. You sleep at the hotel tonight. Then we go in the morning."

There was little sleep that night, though. In our hotel room, we had our introduction to the huge beetles that live in the tropics. Annie was so afraid that one would scuttle over her as she slept, she scarcely closed her eyes. I, for my part, was terrified of one crawling up under my skirt. We got up early, and were very glad to be off.

When we arrived at the boat dock, we found that the family with the two dreadful boys was among our group. They had a huge amount of luggage, including two hatboxes and a large, empty birdcage. The boatman refused to take them with all these things. They argued for a long time, but the boatman would not budge. Finally, they gave in. Suitcases, boxes, and the birdcage were left by the riverside. All the other luggage was piled in the bottom of the boat, and we pushed off. Mrs. Sour Apple was even more sour than before.

The trip was beautiful. As the boatman poled the boat along, we watched the world go by. The air rang with the calls of colorful birds and the chattering of monkeys. Along the banks, the emerald-green jungle was thick. I saw my first palm trees. They swayed gracefully in the wind.

We were five days on the water. It was very hot and damp. At night, we stopped to sleep in airy little huts. A cooler breeze blew. If it had not been for the constant mosquitoes, it would have been fine.

Finally, we could go no farther on the river. It was time to travel on land. This meant about twenty miles of riding on mules. The narrow track was very rough. Mrs. Sour Apple rode sidesaddle, looking very uncomfortable. We did fine, bumping along through the jungle. But on the last day, Mrs. Sour Apple and her husband both grew very feverish. Malaria, said the guides. A very bad disease, indeed.

At last we were in Panama City. Mr. and Mrs. Sour Apple were helped off the boat and immediately taken to a doctor. We would not see them again.

We checked into a small pink hotel on the

main street. While Annie lay down with me to rest on the bed, her father went downstairs to see what he could learn. He was back in an hour. "The news is not very good, I'm afraid," he reported.

"Why not?" asked Annie. She sat up.

"Well, for one thing," he said, "the shipping company lied. There are no ships waiting. There are hundreds of people stranded here. Or thousands, I don't know. They are all waiting for ships to come."

"Oh, my goodness," said Annie. She shook her head, as if to shake off the bad news. "Well, then," she said, "we'll just have to have fun here until a boat comes."

"But there's something else," he said. "They are having an epidemic here. It's a disease called cholera. It can kill you in days, or even in a few hours. I want you to stay in this room. I will go out and try to get us onto a ship. I will bring food back for you. But I must keep you safe."

Annie's face fell. And for the first time, I was really worried.

For the next two weeks, there we were, stuck. Mr. Brown went out every day to try to get us all onto a ship. We stayed in the room, praying that he would not come home sick. The man in the next room must have had cholera, because we began to hear him coughing. We never saw him at all. But the coughing went on, getting worse all the time. Finally, after a few days, it stopped. We did not know if the man was dead or alive. It was just awful.

At last, Mr. Brown burst into the room. "Pack your things, my darling girl!" he said. "We're off to San Francisco on the *Golden Gate!*"

CHAPTER FOUR

San Francisco

The voyage to San Francisco was much better. We did not hit any storms. The ship, however, was jammed with people desperate to get out of Panama. This time, our room had twelve people in it. Annie did not let go of me for one second. And Mr. Brown did not lose sight of Annie for a second, either.

At long last, we reached the harbor at San Francisco. The whole journey had taken three months, not five weeks. It had cost twice as much as it was supposed to. At this rate, Mr. Brown would run out of money soon if he could not find gold.

As we neared shore, we saw something strange. The harbor was jammed with empty ships. They floated at anchor, their sails rolled up, silent as ghost ships.

"Papa," said Annie, "why are there so many empty ships?"

He shaded his eyes to look. "I don't know, Annie," he said. "I don't know."

We soon got our answer. As we approached the shore, our crew started to gather up their things. The captain began shouting at his men. "Let me remind you," he said. "You signed on for the return voyage! You are not to desert this ship!"

"Sorry, Cap'n!" shouted one sailor. "We're off to find gold!"

The harborside was filled with things that people had managed, somehow, to carry this far. There were trunks, chairs, even sofas. But they had all been abandoned. As we soon learned, there was no way to get them to gold country. There were no porters. There were very few carriages to hire. And so, people just left their things behind. We counted ourselves lucky that we did not have much luggage.

Mr. Brown carried the two large suitcases, and Annie took me and a small bag.

We walked the crowded streets, searching for a decent boardinghouse. The streets were muddy and rutted. On every street, we saw miners. Their hair was wild, and their beards were long. Leather pouches of gold dust hung from their belts.

A ragtag bunch of boys ran down the street. Their faces were filthy.

"Where are their parents?" Mr. Brown wondered aloud. "Why are these boys running wild?"

A miner standing nearby heard his question. "They're orphans," he explained. "Lost their parents on the trip across the country. They eat what they can and sleep where they can. Watch out. They'll steal your money if you let them."

"How awful!" said Annie. "No parents at all! Our trip here must have been easy, compared with theirs."

The miner looked at Annie. He smiled. "I left five little girls at home," he said. "I miss them terrible."

"Where are you from?" asked Mr. Brown.

"Maine," the miner replied. "Got here last month."

Maine! My heart jumped when I heard the name. If only I could have gotten some news about my true home! Nobody knew where I came from. It was a secret that would likely remain with me forever. A doll sits quietly and keeps a thousand secrets. And no one ever knows it.

"Have you found much gold?" Mr. Brown asked the miner.

"A fair amount," was the reply. "But it's getting harder. Too many miners. If I was you, I'd go up to the Feather River. I hear there's gold up there."

Mr. Brown shook his hand. "I thank you kindly," he said. "I wish you luck."

"Same to you," said the man.

A rat ran right across our path, and Annie screamed. "Better get used to them," laughed the miner. "There's more of 'em in town than people." Then he patted Annie on the head. "Take good care of your pa," he said. "And your little friend, too," he added, giving me a pat as well.

At last we found a boardinghouse that looked clean. It cost twelve dollars a week. "That includes breakfast," said Mrs. Clark, the owner. "Be downstairs by seven."

"We'll only be here a day or two," said Mr. Brown. "Just enough to rest and figure out how to get up to gold country."

"My son is running people up there by mule," said Mrs. Clark. "You can go with him, if you like. It will cost fifty dollars."

"Fifty!" said Mr. Brown.

"Everything costs more here," she said. "You'll see. There's less of everything. It all has to be brought from somewhere else. A jar of applesauce cost me six dollars yesterday. My son and I have to eat, too."

Annie and her father looked at each other. This trip was not going to get easier.

We waited for Mrs. Clark's son to return. It seemed that there was not going to be a cheaper way to travel, short of walking. That was out of the question for the Browns, though some people did it.

While we waited, Mr. Brown bought the tools he would need for mining. The main items were a shovel, a pickax, and a great round flat pan. He also bought a canvas tent and a few pots and pans and dishes.

While Mr. Brown prepared, Annie could do as she liked. Sometimes she went with him. But most of the time, she preferred to hang about the boardinghouse with me. By now, Annie was beginning to realize how different her life was going to be in California. At home in New York, she was under someone's eye every moment. But here, things were not so orderly. Everyone was on his own here, even the children.

All the talk at the boardinghouse was of gold mining. The miners traded information about all the different camps, or diggings. They talked about whether much gold had been found there. The names of these settlements were like nothing I had ever heard. They were rough names, made up by rough men. There was Slumgullion, Last Chance, and Mad Mule Gulch. There was Poker Flat, You Bet, and Bedbug.

What kinds of places could these be? I wondered.

We were soon to find out, because Mrs. Clark's son Ben returned on the fourth day. I was surprised at how young he was. He could not have been more than thirteen.

"We'll go day after tomorrow," he told us. "Mules need to rest a bit." In truth, he looked as if he needed to rest, too.

At last, we were ready to go. At dawn, Mr. Brown and Ben loaded up the mules. There were four of them in all—one for each person, and one pack mule. Mr. Brown had bought enough food to get us started. There were thirty pounds of flour, and twenty pounds each of rice, beans, and bacon. And there was a large sack of coffee.

Annie's father settled the bill with Mrs. Clark, including Ben's money. We were off.

"Well, Annie," he said as we clip-clopped out of town, "there's no turning back now. We have

twenty-eight dollars left. We'd better find some gold."

"We will, Papa," said Annie. "We will."

The trip took five days. We followed the Sacramento River north to the Feather River. At night, we simply slept in bedrolls on the ground. Annie hugged me and looked up at the millions of stars.

"Look at them all, Hitty!" she whispered to me. "We could hardly see any stars in New York. Did you ever see anything like this in your life?"

I had, of course. The sky over Maine was just as beautiful. I lay in Annie's arms, remembering it.

Finally, after traveling a good two hundred miles, we began climbing into the Sierra Nevada Mountains. The country was very rugged here.

"We can go as far up the river as you want," said Ben. "Poverty Hill is just ahead."

Poverty Hill! I prayed we would not end

up in a place with a name like that.

"What's after Poverty Hill?" asked Mr. Brown, perhaps thinking the same thing.

"Whiskey Flat," Ben replied.

"Whiskey Flat?" said Annie. "I heard the miners talking about that camp. They said there was still gold to be found there. Can we go there, Papa?"

Mr. Brown hesitated. "I don't like the name so much," he said.

"It's better than Poverty Hill," Annie reminded him.

"So it is," her father agreed. "All right, Ben. Whiskey Flat it is."

And so, the next afternoon, our little mule train pulled into Whiskey Flat. Like all the mining camps, it was beside the river. To reach it, we had to go down a hillside so steep that we feared the mules would tumble forward.

We could hear the sounds of gold mining

long before we reached the town. There was the murmur of voices as the men worked. There was the *chink* of spades into the river gravel, and the rattle of the gravel in the pans. And over it all, there was the constant rushing of water.

Finally, we were there. It was not really a town, just a collection of tents and shacks. There was a sort of street that went through it—just a dusty track, really. We led the mules toward the edge of the camp.

"Here," said Mr. Brown, spotting a flat place a short distance away from a rough shack. "This is where we will pitch our tent."

Annie put me down on a rock and helped unload the mules. When they were done, Mr. Brown shook Ben's hand and gave Ben two of his precious dollars. Ben thanked him, and then he was off.

And there we were. Our new home was Whiskey Flat, California.

CHAPTER FIVE

The Quest for Gold

It took Mr. Brown and Annie two hours and a good deal of frustration to get the tent up. By the time they were done, they were almost staggering with tiredness.

"I'll make us some beans and rice," said Mr. Brown. "Then we'll go to sleep."

"I'll watch you cook," said Annie. "I need to learn." She yawned.

"Can you see if there's some firewood about?" said her father. "If you'll do that, I'll fetch some water."

Annie took me along for courage. The sun

was going down now, and the shadows were long. There was not a soul nearby.

There was plenty of firewood, though. Pretty soon, Annie had a big armful, with me perched on top.

As she neared the tent, we heard voices. Her father was talking to someone. Who could it be?

Mr. Brown was sitting on a stump and chatting with the biggest man I had ever seen. He looked about seven feet tall. His brown hair was long and wild, and so was his beard.

"Annie," said Mr. Brown, "meet our next-door neighbor. This is Pete. He comes from Pennsylvania."

Annie put down the firewood. She could not take her eyes off the man. "My friends call me Big Pete," the man said in a booming voice. He extended his huge hand to Annie. "Pleased to meet you, little miss."

"How do you do," said Annie. She looked up

at Big Pete's face as she might have looked up at a treetop.

"All the men will be very excited to have a child here," said Pete. "There're no other children about. Everyone left the young 'uns home with the wives. I have three at home. Just waitin' for me to come home loaded with gold." He guffawed.

"In our case, leaving Annie behind was impossible," Mr. Brown explained. "So here we are. My little forty-niner and I."

"And very welcome you are!" Pete told Annie. "We'll all look after you real well."

"Thank you kindly for that," said Mr. Brown. "This is some pretty rough country for a girl. I did not realize how rough."

"She'll fit right in," said Pete. "I can tell she's got gumption."

"That I do," Annie said proudly. "And so does Hitty." She held me out to show me to Pete.

"Well, I'll be jiggered," he said. "All the way from New York to California. I guess Hitty does have the stuff. Well, we'll take care of her, too."

With some difficulty, Annie and Mr. Brown got a fire going. Pete brought over a bit of salt pork he had, and they all sat down to a pretty good dinner.

After dinner, Mr. Brown turned to Annie. "How would you feel about singing a song for us? I miss your voice so. I know there's no piano, but—"

Annie stood up. "I'd love to sing," she said. "If you'll join in. This is our new home, and our new home should have music."

"Amen to that!" said Pete.

So Annie sang. Even without the piano, it sounded wonderful. First she did "Froggie Went A-Courtin'," which made Pete laugh. Then she sang "Down in the Valley." "Down in the valley, valley so low/Hang your head over, hear the wind blow," went the sad lyrics.

Pete wiped away a tear. "That was beautiful," he said. "You have such a pretty voice. I'll bet the other boys would like to hear it, too."

"I love to sing," said Annie. "We can sing anytime."

At last, Pete stood up. "I'm just as tired as an old mule," he said. "Time to get some sleep. In the morning," he told Mr. Brown, "I'll take you down to the river. I'll introduce you around, and show you how to pan for gold. All right?"

"That would be much appreciated," said Mr. Brown.

When the three tin dishes had been washed, it was time to go to sleep.

Annie woke up just after dawn. She opened the tent flap and took me outside. It was going to be a beautiful, warm May day. She stretched and yawned.

Soon her father emerged, blinking in the sun. "I'm ready to go find some gold!" he replied. "A night of sleep has done me a world of good!"

"And I'm ready to help," said Annie.

"After you've done your lessons for the day," he reminded her. "Just because there is no school here, it does not mean we'll neglect your lessons."

"I know, Papa. I know," she said. They had brought books on science, mathematics, and literature all the way from New York. That was their bargain: If she was going to California, she would have to keep up her studies. They had always dreamed that Annie would go to college one day. Very few women did, but Annie was determined.

But first, there was breakfast.

"Well," said Mr. Brown, "what should we have? Rice and beans?"

"Or perhaps beans and rice?" said Annie. They laughed.

Annie helped her father build a fire and make

breakfast. Just as they were finishing, Big Pete showed up. "Ready?" he asked.

"Ready," Mr. Brown responded. He buttoned on his suspenders.

Pete looked at their breakfast. "When you get tired of rice and beans, by the way," he said, "you can go to the slop shop. You'll need some fruit now and then. Don't want to get scurvy. Ryan has most everything in there. It's not a fancy store, but it'll do. It's just yonder down the street."

"What's scurvy?" asked Annie.

"It's a disease you get from not eating fruit. You get boils on your gums. Then your teeth fall out," Pete explained. Annie gasped.

"Are things as expensive there as in San Francisco?" Mr. Brown asked Pete.

"Worse," Pete said with a grin. Mr. Brown looked worried.

"Let's go strike it rich," said Pete. He hoisted his tools onto his shoulder.

"May I come down and help you when I'm done studying?" Annie asked.

"I'll be happy to see you," Mr. Brown replied. "You can tell me what you learned. And maybe you can sing me a song to pass the time."

The men trudged off. Annie put me down on a rock. Then she got out her mathematics book, some paper, her quill pen, and ink. To keep herself company, she read me her sums as she worked. "Four hundred eighty-three plus nine hundred seventy-eight," she said. "This is a hard one, Hitty. I wish you could help me."

Finally, she was done. She closed the book. "And now," she said, "we can look for Papa!"

We followed the sound of the river. In a couple of minutes we were there. It was a beautiful river, swollen with the melted snow of spring.

And everywhere there were men, a hundred or more, all working hard. Some had large pans, like Mr. Brown's. Some used strange-looking wooden boxes that they rocked like cradles. One man had a large laundry tub. The men all lifted their heads to look at Annie as she passed. Some smiled. Others waved.

Annie's father was at the far end of the group. He was standing up to his knees in the river water. His face was running with sweat. Big Pete was working beside him. When he saw Annie, Mr. Brown straightened up and waved to her.

Annie ran to the edge of the water. She sat down and took off her high-button leather shoes. "Did you find any gold?" she called to her father.

"Not yet," he called back.

Before she could wade in, Big Pete and her father came out to join her. Then she noticed that the other men were coming out of the water, too. "Fellows," said Pete in his booming voice, "I want you to meet someone. This is Miss Annie Brown."

All the men clustered around Annie and me. Some of them put out mud-covered hands to shake. Annie looked as if she had never been the center of so much attention in her life. I certainly hadn't, for the men made a great fuss over me as well. It had been so long since they had seen a child, or even a doll. They all missed their families. Most of them were three thousand miles away, in another world, it seemed.

Finally, the fussing was over. The men had to return to their work. They were there for one thing only: to make money and get out.

Annie set me down on the hot sand to watch. Then she hitched up her skirt and waded into the water. "My goodness, it's cold!" she gasped.

"You'll get used to it," said her father. "And you can stop whenever you want."

"I want to help," she said determinedly.

Panning for gold did not take much skill. Mr. Brown had learned it that morning from Pete.

Now he showed Annie how to do it. "First," he said, "we put the pan down on the bottom. We'll use the shovel to put in a big load of rocks and gravel." He bent down and demonstrated. "We stir it around underwater and let the big stones pour off." Annie bent down and stirred the stones in the icy water.

Now her father brought the pan up. "We'll just keep doing the same thing," he said. "Stirring and pouring, stirring and pouring. The gold is heavier than the stones, so it will sink to the bottom. Those wooden rockers are easier, I hear. Maybe I will be able to buy one soon." He put some water in the pan and shook it around. Annie swirled the gravel with her hand, helping it to float out.

"Pete tells me it will get easier in the summer," he told her. "The river is lower."

Finally there was just sand at the bottom. "See anything in there?" he asked.

She looked closely. "Yes!" she cried. "Look, it's a little nugget!"

Her father hugged her. They were both covered in mud and sweat. But they did not care. "You've brought me luck!" he cried. "My lucky girl!"

Annie waded to shore. She put the nugget into my lap for safekeeping. I had never had gold in my lap, I can tell you!

They kept working. Annie sang songs to pass the time. The other men kept looking up from their work. They would smile when they heard their favorite songs. Often, they tipped their hats to her.

The work did not stop until it was too dark to see. By that time, my skirt was full of gold nuggets! Annie tied my skirt up around them. I was so proud to be holding the gold, I did not even mind my petticoat showing. And besides, here in gold country, ladies were not very formal.

As they all walked up the hill to the camp, the men spoke to Annie. "That was beautiful," said one. "It reminded me of home," said another. "It made the work go faster, too," said a third.

Annie hugged me. I could tell she was glad to have spread so much cheer.

CHAPTER SIX

My Terrible Ride

After they had cleaned up and changed, Annie and her father tied their gold into a clean handkerchief.

"Let's go buy ourselves a wonderful dinner," said Mr. Brown. "No rice and beans for us tonight. Pete says Mr. Ryan keeps the shop open in the evening for the miners."

"Oh, maybe we can get some oranges!" cried Annie. "And cake! And some chicken. And greens. And eggs. We need eggs." She was counting on her fingers. "I guess we'll be able to buy enough food for the whole summer with this gold!"

Annie scooped me up, and we set off. She skipped down the dirt path ahead of her father. The men waved from their campfires. "There goes our little songbird!" called one of them.

The slop shop's name suited the place very well. It was a dark, cramped shack. It smelled of mildew. But Mr. Ryan did have things to sell. There were bags of potatoes and onions. And there were preserved meats, like salt pork and jerked beef.

"Welcome, newcomers," said Mr. Ryan. He was a thin, pale man with circles under his eyes. "What can I get you?"

"Well," said Mr. Brown, "we have a nice amount of gold, and we aim to do a lot of shopping."

"Let's see what you have there," said Mr. Ryan.

Mr. Brown put the handkerchief on the counter and untied it. With a sharp eye, the store-keeper sized it up. "Looks like just about an even ounce," he said. "Let's put it on the scale and see."

The scale had two flat pans that balanced each other. On one pan, he placed the gold. On the other, he set a small metal weight. The two pans were perfectly even. "Just as I thought," said Mr. Ryan with a satisfied smile. "Exactly an ounce. That's worth sixteen dollars."

"Sixteen dollars!" said Mr. Brown. "That's all?"

"That's what the bank in Sacramento gives me. Sixteen dollars. So that's what I give you," said Mr. Ryan. "I could charge extra for my trouble, but I don't."

Mr. Brown could hardly believe it. "I thought for sure it would be worth more," he said.

"Afraid not," said Ryan. It seemed he had heard this many times before. "Now, what can I get you?"

"Well," said Mr. Brown, "we thought we'd buy some oranges and some eggs. Some canned sardines would be nice. And we could use some butter. And—"

"Stop right there," said the storekeeper. "A can of sardines, that's twelve dollars right there. A dozen eggs, that's ten. Can't get butter. Haven't had oranges in weeks. I have a lot of hardtack, though. That's cheap. And I have a fair stock of potatoes. A dollar a pound."

"A dollar a pound!" sputtered Mr. Brown. "Why, they cost me a penny a pound in New York!"

"Nobody has to bring them down a mountain on a mule to New York," replied Mr. Ryan.

"What's hardtack?" asked Annie. "Maybe we should get some, if it's cheap."

Mr. Ryan handed her a round sort of cracker. "I see why it's called *hard*tack," she said, trying to bite it.

"All right, we'll just have to make some choices," said Mr. Brown. "No sardines, that's for sure."

In the end, we walked home with half a

dozen eggs, three big potatoes, and a large piece of cheese that was only a bit moldy. And, of course, a lot of hardtack.

"It's all right, Papa," said Annie. "We'll do better tomorrow."

But they did not do better the next day. Once again, Mr. Brown ended the day with about an ounce of gold.

Big Pete came over for a pot-luck dinner again. "From what I hear," he said, "things were very good last year, at the beginning. You could just pry up lumps of gold with your pocket-knife. But it's already been picked over. The nuggets are smaller. In a few months, or a year, there will not be much left. People will be working all day for a little dust."

"If only things didn't cost so much," said Mr. Brown.

"If only," Pete agreed. "I have half a mind to

quit mining and open a little store instead."

"I think you might just do better that way," said Mr. Brown.

The next day, Annie read all morning. Then she took me down to the river to join her father. She put me down in the sand. Then she looked at me. "I think you need to come in the water today," she said to me. "I think you're lonely out here."

So she picked me up and carried me into the river with her. "Are you sure you should have Hitty here?" her father asked.

"I'll be careful," she replied. "I'll stir the rocks with one hand."

Annie began to work with her father. I cannot say I was not a bit nervous. The water rushed along, making eddies around her. Sometimes she let my feet dangle into the water. It was shockingly cold.

And then . . . disaster! In one careless second,

I was dropped into the water. Annie screamed. She tried to catch me, but it was too late. "Hitty!" I heard her shriek.

Mr. Brown dropped his pan and lunged for me. But I was already rushing downstream in the freezing water. I whirled about, helpless.

And now I heard a new noise. It came from somewhere ahead of me. It was louder than the rushing of the river. It was more of a roar. A waterfall!

Suddenly, I felt my dress snag on something. What had stopped me? I saw that it was a tree branch that had fallen into the river. Now it was wedged among some rocks. As long as my dress held, I was safe. But sooner or later, it would have to tear. And then I would be shooting toward the waterfall.

All at once, I saw a large shape on the riverbank nearby. It was Big Pete! He plunged into the river and came crashing toward me.

Meanwhile, I could feel my dress ripping. Would he reach me in time, or would I just whirl away from him?

He stretched his enormous hand out toward me, and . . . he had me! A large piece tore out of my dress as he pulled me free, but I did not care. I was safe.

Annie, by this time, had caught up to Pete. He waded back to shore and handed me to her. "Oh, Pete," she sobbed, "you saved her! I lost her, and you saved her! How can I ever thank you?"

He grinned. "Just sing me a couple of songs," he said.

That night after supper, Annie gave a special concert, just for Pete. I sat on a stump near the fire.

"What would you like to hear?" Annie asked Pete.

"Do you know 'Sweet Betsy from Pike'?" he said.

"Of course! I love it." Annie began to sing the popular Gold Rush tune.

Pete and Mr. Brown joined in for the chorus: "Good-bye, Pike County, farewell for a while—we'll come back again when we've panned out our pile."

"That was wonderful!" said a voice nearby. It was one of the younger miners. He had come over to listen.

"Why, thank you!" said Annie. She looked into the darkness and discovered that several other men had joined the group.

"Miss Annie?" asked one of them. "Could you sing me 'Shenandoah'? My wife used to sing it, and I miss her terrible. I'd be pleased to give you a little nugget of gold if you'd sing it."

"Oh, you don't have to do that," said Annie. "I love to sing."

"It would bring me a lot of happiness," he

said. "I'd love to give you a bit of somethin'. There's precious little that's nice to spend it on around here."

"Papa, may I take it?" Annie asked. "I could save it for college."

"Well, then, all right," said her father. "It's for a good cause."

Annie's eyes shone as she took the nugget. "I'll do the best job I can," she promised.

As soon as she began to sing, all the men joined in. "Oh, Shenandoah, I long to hear you / Away, you rolling river / Away, I'm bound away / 'Cross the wide Missouri." Several of the men wiped tears out of their beards when they were done.

"Let's have a happy one now!" said another man. "I'll give a pinch of dust for 'Skip to My Lou.' Do you know it?"

"Of course," said Annie.

And so, the whole evening was spent in song.

Annie had a fine time, and so did the men. When it was time to go to sleep, Annie snuggled down beside me in the bedroll. She held her mother's red silk bag. "Look in here," she whispered to me. She opened the drawstring so I could see. "Now we're forty-niners, too, Hitty."

CHAPTER SEVEN

A Surprise in the Woods

Spring gave way to summer. The river did get lower. But Mr. Brown never seemed to get ahead. Almost everything he made went into buying food.

"I don't know if this is worth it, Annie," he told her one night. "But it took us so much to get here. And what will people say if we come home with nothing?" He rubbed his sore knuckles. Like many of the other miners, he was getting painful rheumatism from the cold water.

"Why should we care what people say?" said Annie. "If they're smart, they'll say we were brave. We took a chance. Mama would approve."

"Yes," he said, smiling tiredly. "I think she would."

"Besides, we may yet strike it rich. You never know."

"The fellows say it gets pretty rough in winter here," he said. "There's heavy rain, and sometimes snow. Most of them plan to spend the winter in Sacramento, and then come back. Maybe we should give it till fall, and then take stock."

"That sounds good," Annie replied.

The next day, Annie finished her reading early. It was quite hot. I sat on the ground in my tattered dress.

"Do you know what, Hitty?" she said to me. "I think we need to go exploring." With that, she swept me up, and we were off. Annie was in her bare feet. It was too hot to wear shoes.

We made our way through the woods. It was

very quiet. Only the knocking of a distant wood-pecker intruded.

Then my dress caught on a bush. "Drat!" said Annie. "Let's see what you're—my goodness, what's this?" She bent down to look more closely.

"Hitty," she cried, "you're a genius!" Her fingers were carefully freeing me from what had caught me fast: thorns. "You've found a raspberry bush!" she said. "Look—black raspberries!" She did a little dance of joy. "And look! There are more bushes everywhere! More berries! Enough to keep us all from getting scurvy!"

Annie excitedly began picking the berries. Faster and faster she went. The juice of the berries made her fingers red. She piled the berries up on the ground.

She filled her apron with the berries. "We'll come back tomorrow," she told me. "With a nice big pot!" And then, holding up her berry-filled apron, she ran back to the camp.

That evening at dinnertime, she stepped onto the dirt track with a large pan and a tin spoon. Her apron was stained red. She began banging on the pan as hard as she could. "Raspberries!" she sang out. "Get your berries here! Only a dollar a cup!"

In moments, the men started coming down the track. They began lining up to buy them. "Raspberries!" everyone said. "What a wonder!" "It's a miracle!" "I haven't had fruit in six months!"

By this time, Annie was quite good at knowing what a dollar's worth of gold looked like. She had been shopping with her father enough times. The men were very happy to give up a small nugget for the forgotten taste of berries.

Annie kept singing and picking berries all summer. Her red bag grew full.

Meanwhile, things were changing in the

camp, and not for the better. Some of the miners had left, and others had come to take their places. Of the ones who left, some went home in disgust. Others decided to try different trades. Big Pete went to San Francisco to open a store. He sold supplies to the new miners. The miner who liked "Shenandoah" had been a barber at home. He began traveling around, cutting hair for two dollars. There were certainly plenty of men who needed haircuts.

Some of the new men were a rowdy lot. In the evenings, Annie and Mr. Brown could hear laughing, cursing, and sometimes fighting from the other end of the camp. Annie began sticking closer to her father.

One afternoon in October, two black men showed up at the river. Annie was panning with her father. The newcomers put their shovels into the riverbank to stake their claims. That was the rule in Whiskey Flat. Anybody who staked a claim could have forty feet of river to work.

But a group of the newer miners came running toward them. "These diggings are for white people!" one of them yelled. "No Negroes, no Indians, no Chinese, no Mexicans! Move off!"

The black men started to move away.

"Now, fellows," Mr. Brown said to the white group, "there's gold enough for all of us. Why don't we—"

"No, there ain't!" snarled the man. "And if you don't want to cause trouble for yourself *and* them, you'll let them go."

The black men were already leaving. There was nothing for Annie's father to do but give up. "You should be ashamed," he said to the white men.

Toward November, the rains came. At first it only rained every few days. Then Annie's father was panning in the rain every other day. The camp was a sea of mud. It was impossible to keep it out of the tent.

Annie and I stayed in the tent when it rained. She needed the lamp to read. But she did not like to do it for long. Lamp oil cost money.

One evening, Annie and Mr. Brown were finishing a soggy dinner. They huddled near the fire for warmth. All at once, Mr. Brown stood up. "What do you say we call it quits?" he said.

"All right," said Annie. "I'll put out the fire. I wouldn't mind going to bed."

"I don't mean going to bed," he said. "I mean leaving. Are you as tired of all this as I am?"

Annie looked at her shoes. They had big holes in them. Then she looked at my shredded dress. "Yes, Papa!" she cried. "I am! I didn't really know it. But what I'd give to sleep in a real bed with a pillow!"

He sat down again. "Then it's settled," he said. "But what shall we do? I don't think we have enough gold to get back to New York. And I don't relish taking that trip again, either."

"Papa, what if we just stayed in San Francisco? Then we'd have no more snowy winters, ever."

"Hmmm," he mused. "We have no close relatives back East, after all. And I hear San Francisco is becoming a very nice city."

"But what would we do there?"

Annie's father thought about that. "You know," he said, "the city is growing so fast. I'm sure they don't have enough schools there. Maybe I could start one. And perhaps I could raise enough money to educate those orphans who roam the streets."

"Papa, what a wonderful idea! Let's do it!"

"The problem is, how? I would have to find some way of working for a living right away. It might be years before I can get the school running."

Annie stood up and went into the tent. She returned with the red bag. "Here, Papa," she said. "This should help."

Mr. Brown's eyes grew wide. "I had no idea you had so much gold!" he cried. She put the bag into his hand. "Why, you must have four pounds here!"

"I'd say it's four and a half," said Annie.

"All this is just from singing and berries?"

"Yes, sir!" she said proudly.

"But, Annie," he said, "we can't use this. This money is for college."

"Right now, our life is more important," she said. "I want to leave here, and so do you. Let's use it to live on while you start the school."

"I don't know—"

"You know I'm right," said Annie.

Her father sighed. "Of course you are. You're always right. But I swear to you, I will work every day until you are old enough to go to college. I will send you."

"I know you will, Papa," she said. And she kissed the top of his head.

CHAPTER EIGHT

Life Changes Again

Six months later, Annie and her father and I were living in a nice house on Fulton Street in San Francisco. They did not have a lot of furniture yet. But they did have a nice upright piano.

The Brown School for Children had seventy students, including Annie and fourteen orphans. There were three teachers. Mr. Brown was still raising money, which was not too difficult. There were plenty of people who had gotten rich in the early Gold Rush months. And there were also many who had gotten rich selling things to the miners. One of them was Big

Pete. He lived around the corner, and they saw him often. His family would be joining him soon, and his children would attend Mr. Brown's school.

Annie had a lovely soft bed and a feather pillow. She had new shoes and a frilly red umbrella. She was taking piano lessons.

And me? I had a brand-new blue satin dress, and a matching hat. I was ready for whatever would come next.

ABOUT THE GOLD RUSH

In the end, the Gold Rush brought some people great wealth, and others only pain. Though a few of the first miners did find huge amounts of gold, most others worked hard and found little. But, like Big Pete, many discovered that they could make a better living in other ways. They started businesses to serve the miners.

For the people who were already living in California, the discovery of gold was a terrible disaster. About 150,000 Native Americans lived there before 1848. Twelve years later, there were only 30,000. The rest had been killed, kidnapped, or starved. There were also thousands of Spanish-speaking people called *Californios*. Most of them were ranchers. The gold miners threw them off their ranches and took their land, destroying their way of life.

Many slaves were brought to California to find gold for their masters. Some free African-Americans also went west, and a few bought freedom for their relatives. And thousands of people who came all the way from China had heard about "the Gold Mountain." They, too, often ended up in businesses.

By the time it was all over, gold had changed the face of California forever. It created the growing state that still exists today.